Momma, Can I Sleep with You Tonight?

HELPING CHILDREN COPE WITH THE IMPACT OF COVID-19

JENNY DELACRUZ

ILLUSTRATIONS BY DANKO HERRERA

This book is dedicated to

all of the children around the globe.

"Momma, can I sleep with you tonight?"

"Of course, son. What's wrong?"

"My whole life feels like a bad dream. I feel too many feelings. They're all twisted up."

"I feel many feelings, too, son. I'm still in shock.

Our lives changed so quickly.

The world we knew just stopped.

But now we have to work together to live in this new one."

"I don't want to believe that COVID-19 is real!"

"Trust me, son, I don't either.

Many people are worried about getting sick. And we worry about the people we care about."

"Momma, I miss my friends and going to the park.

I miss riding my bike to the ice cream shop. Sometimes, I get so mad I could just burst!"

"Son, I feel the same way.

It's frustrating when what's familiar is taken away. But we can look forward to the day when we can do these fun things again. If I went to the ice cream shop, I'd get a chocolate sundae. What about you?"

"A vanilla cone with sprinkles!"

"Momma, what can I do to make it end? What if I pray every day? What if I eat my peas?

I just want things to go back to normal!"

"Son, I do, too. The good news is that scientists are working hard to find the best treatment and a vaccine."

"I can't stop feeling sad.

I miss Nana's hugs and her good stories, but I don't want her to get sick.

My stomach feels like it's full of knots."

"I miss Nana, too, but we're doing the right thing by keeping our distance. We cannot see Nana in person, but we can call her or have a video chat."

"I guess—but Momma?"

"Yes, son?"

"I just feel so scared."

"Those do look scary. But they're the same people behind them. The masks keep everyone safe because it stops the spread of the virus. Remember, there are many places where people wear protective gear to keep us all safe, like our dentist and doctor's mask and gloves."

"What about the loud sirens? I hear them all the time now."

"That can be scary, I know. But remember, when you hear a siren, it means help is on its way."

"Maybe when I'm big, I can help, too!"

"Yes. Actually, you can help now by washing your hands, keeping good distance, and sneezing into your elbow. Remember that you're not alone. I'm always here to talk to you, but sometimes, it helps to talk to someone else, too. Would you like to do that?"

"I'm not sure. I just want to know if I'm ever going to feel happy again."

"I am sure you will. But there are lots of ways to be happy.

It doesn't always mean that the hard things go away.

It means that we learn to deal with our feelings and take small steps forward."

"Like what?"

"Well, how about we make our own ice cream shop until we can go out again?"

"In our own house?"

"Yes, in our own house."

"I can't wait! Momma, let's write down everything we need!"

"Son, let's get some sleep first. We can do that first thing tomorrow, okay?"

"Okay. But can I still sleep with you tonight?"

AFTERWORD

It's important as we support ourselves and young minds to be aware of the stages of grief and loss. Many of us have lost loved ones due to COVID-19, and the majority of us are dealing with the loss of the normalcy we once had in our lives. The stages of grief are:

- ➢ Denial
- ➢ Anger
- ➢ Bargaining
- ➢ Sadness/depression
- ➢ Acceptance

Denial can manifest as shock and numbness.

Anger can present as restlessness or an increase of temper tantrums or angry outbursts.

Bargaining is children behaving in ways to try to make the situation better. It can stem from the belief that they are somehow responsible for the cause of grief.

Sadness and depression can be seen as tiredness and boredom.

Acceptance comes in bursts as children grieve in short periods of time.

These stages are not linear and, therefore, it's natural for children to have mood swings and shift to different stages on any given day.

If children ask questions, make sure to respond honestly and give them age-appropriate responses. The key is to do this while helping them to find ways to hope in the future. You can also encourage children to express their emotions and articulate how they are feeling through the tools of art and play. For example, you can ask them to draw a picture of how they are feeling. Make sure to be intentional about taking moments to play with them while checking in. Children are more likely to be expressive while playing.

It's important to note that children may not display the stages of grief for up to a year. Even if they are not displaying any signs of grief, it's important to ask questions about how they are feeling regarding the changes in their lives so they feel safe to share, rather than suffer in silence.

RESOURCES

A Little Hope – The National Foundation for Grieving Children Teens and Families

www.alittlehope.org

Conscious Discipline – COVID-19: Resources for Families and Educators

consciousdiscipline.com

The Dougy Center – The National Center for Grieving Families & Children

www.dougy.org/grief-resources/help-for-kids

National Alliance for Grieving Children

childrengrieve.org/resources/covid-19-resources

Grief.com

grief.com

ABOUT THE AUTHOR

Jenny Delacruz, M.S. is a licensed counselor specializing in family conflicts, trauma, and parenting issues. Jenny is also a philanthropist who advocates for human rights; her work focuses on promoting diversity. Her passion for teaching her children about world history and current events led her to pursue writing and launch her own educational children's book series.

If you want more of Jenny Delacruz's work, check out her first book, Fridays with Ms. Mélange: Haiti. She has a YouTube channel called Storytime with Ms. Mélange where she reads diverse children's books aloud. You can also visit her online at www.cobbscreekpublishing.com.

ABOUT THE ILLUSTRATOR

Danko draws his inspiration from nature and landscapes. He is versatile in many drawing styles through his poetic and detailed use of colors and lines.

He has worked for various environmental, educational, and commercial organizations and businesses as an illustrator, and his art has also appeared in best-seller books, murals, and even in art festivals around the world in countries like Denmark, Argentina, the United States, and Mexico.

Visit his website at danko.mx, and follow him on Instagram @danko.mx.